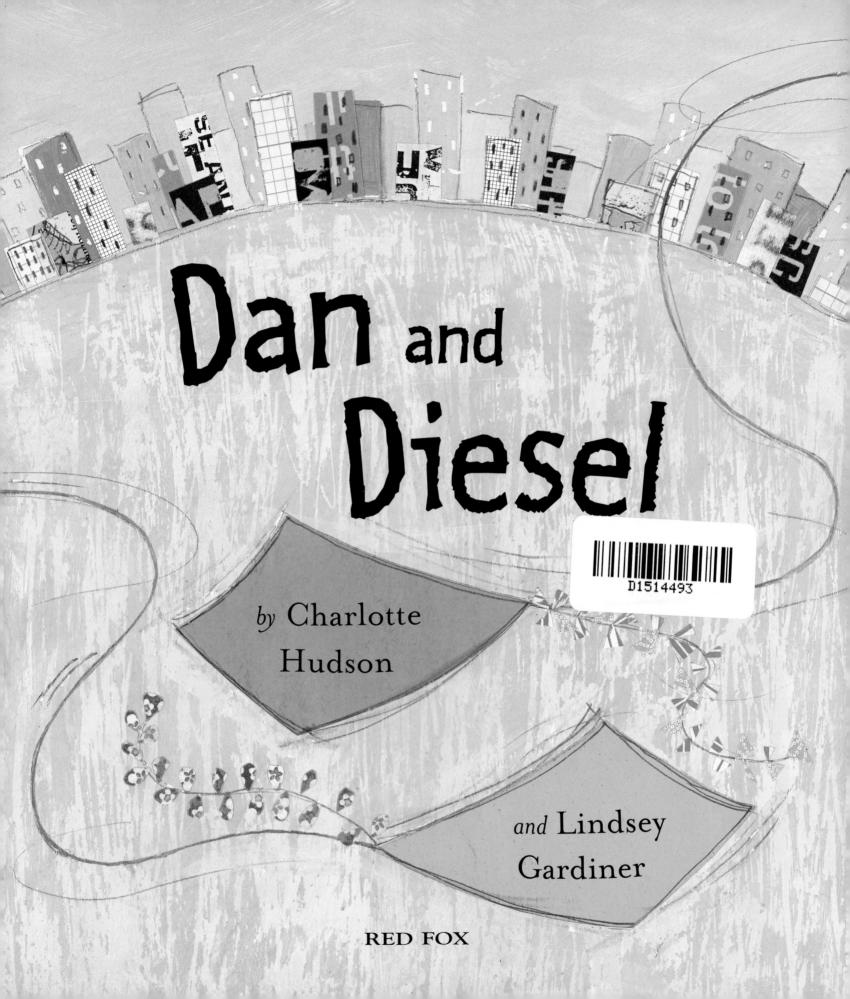

Dan and Diesel

by Charlotte Hudson

and Lindsey Gardiner

RED FOX

My brother Dan
has a dog.

He is a

WONDER ⭐ **DOG!**

He can do

anything!

He can ride on trains and planes
and in underground tunnels.

He can stand next to an **enormous** fire-breathing dragon

ROAR

and **never** flinch an inch.

My brother's dog is called
Diesel because he is jet black.
Dan and Diesel
do everything together.

They play **Jazz** together
in the **Boogaloo** band.

They'd go to the moon

and back together if they could.

And every evening when they get home, while I have
my tea, Diesel snuggles into his special place.
It's warm and soft and smells

oh so *wonderful.*

It's the place
his nose fits in,
just by Dan's leg.

You could put Diesel in the middle of a field of rabbits but he wouldn't leave this place.

You could throw him balls and "go fetch them" boomerangs, but he'd turn the other cheek.

My brother means more to him than any of these things.

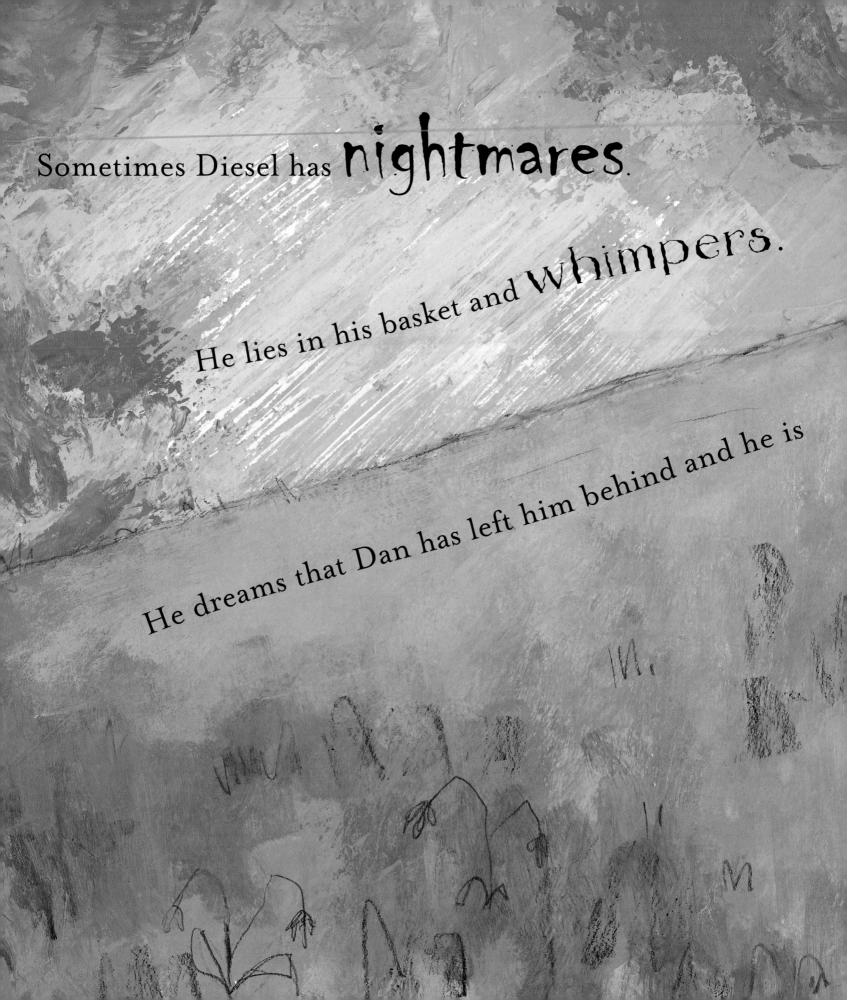

Sometimes Diesel has **nightmares**.

He lies in his basket and whimpers.

He dreams that Dan has left him behind and he is

miles away from his special place.

A world without Dan would look like this to Diesel.

And sometimes my brother has **nightmares.** He dreams that Diesel has got lost, or somehow whisked away.

A world without Diesel would look like this to Dan.

Then one day, Diesel really does get whisked away.

The "whiskers" have a big black van
and sell wonder dogs
for lots of money!

BAD - 1

Dan tries to be brave,

but he doesn't much feel like conquering the world on his own.

I'm sure that Diesel's trying to be brave too, but he's never been this far from his special place before.

All night Dan waits up while the dog squad search the city.

I creep down in my pyjamas and try to cheer him up with a *boogaloo* tune,

but nothing seems to work.

The next day,
Dan can't cross
the city to the
Swingtime Café.

Then I remind my brother. Diesel is a **wonder dog.**

MISSING
"WONDER DOG"

Please contact

2789 46501

REWARD

He can . . .

He can . . . .

sniff sniff

STOP!! POLICE!!

POLICE

. . . and summon help.

JAZZ LIVE BANDS . . .

He can smel

It feels like a lifetime apart, but at last,

Dan and Diesel are back together!

Diesel sits by Dan's leg and watches the world
and Dan feels the world all around him.

Together, they can do anything.
Together, my brother says, they can conquer the world!

For Sarah, through all the years — Charlotte
For John, together we can do anything — Lindsey xx

With thanks to
The Guide Dogs for the Blind Association

DAN AND DIESEL
A RED FOX BOOK 978 1 849 41211 7

First published in Great Britain in 2006 by Red Fox,
an imprint of Random House Children's Books
Originated by The Bodley Head

7 9 10 8 6

Red Fox Books are published by Random House Children's Books,
61–63 Uxbridge Road, London W5 5SA,
a division of The Random House Group Ltd

Addresses for companies within The Random House Group Limited can be found
at: www.randomhouse.co.uk/offices.htm

THE RANDOM HOUSE GROUP Limited Reg. No. 954009
www.kidsatrandomhouse.co.uk

A CIP catalogue record for this book is available from the British Library.

Printed in Singapore